Rose or Thorn?

By Susan Taylor Shupe

Illustrated by Trice Boerens

AuthorHouse™
1663 Liberty Drive
Bloomington, IN 47403
www.authorhouse.com
Phone: 833-262-8899

Because of the dynamic nature of the Internet, any web addresses or links contained in
this book may have changed since publication and may no longer be valid. The views
expressed in this work are solely those of the author and do not necessarily reflect the views
of the publisher, and the publisher hereby disclaims any responsibility for them.

Any people depicted in stock imagery provided by Getty Images are models,
and such images are being used for illustrative purposes only.
Certain stock imagery © Getty Images.

This book is printed on acid-free paper.

Interior Image Credit: Trice Boerens

ISBN: 978-1-6655-7424-2 (sc)
ISBN: 978-1-6655-7425-9 (hc)
ISBN: 978-1-6655-7426-6 (e)

Library of Congress Control Number: 2022919673

Print information available on the last page.

Published by AuthorHouse 10/22/2022

authorHOUSE

When you touch the thorn on a rose, it feels sharp to your finger.

When you touch the pedal on a rose, it feels nice to your finger.

A girl named Thorn

lives next door to a
girl named Rose.

Thorn and her brother
often say mean things.

When someone says
something mean, it feels
sharp to your heart.

Saying mean things to others
makes them feel unhappy.
Your finger has feelings
and so does your heart.

You shouldn't touch something that will hurt your finger. You shouldn't say something that will hurt someone's heart.

Rose and her brother
often say kind things.

When someone says
something kind, it feels
nice to your heart.

Saying nice things to others makes them feel happy. Say to others what you would want them to say to you.

One day when Thorn and her brother said something mean, Rose crossed her arms and calmly asked, "How would you feel if I said that to you?"

Then she turned around
and walked away.

The next day, Thorn and her brother said they were sorry. That made each of them feel happy.

Now they are
good friends

who like to say and
also do nice things.

Doing nice things
for others

makes them feel happy.

When a new family moved
into the neighborhood,

Rose and Thorn invited them to play tetherball.

When their neighbor dropped a bunch of oranges on her driveway,

their brothers helped
her pick them up and put
them in her basket.

Rose and Thorn and their brothers like to surprise an elderly couple who live on the corner by bringing them roses from their mothers' gardens.

They carefully remove the thorns so no one gets hurt.

They also like to
make cards

to give to their teachers,
family and friends.

At the end
of the day,

they feel happy when they
think about something
they said or did to
make someone happy.

Saying and doing nice things
makes us feel happy, too.

Printed in the United States
by Baker & Taylor Publisher Services